This little adventure book
belongs to

· · · · · · ·

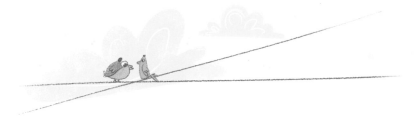

ISBN: 978-0-6455604-0-4

The *Adventures*
of
HERBERT FIGMONT MOPPITY ZOO-BOP
Herbert and the Golden Eagle

by April Moon

illustrated by Roksolana Panchyshyn

Exciting events rarely happened on Herbert's trip to school.

His mom had packed his peanut butter and jelly sandwich lunch

as usual and kissed him goodbye before he walked to the bus stop.

"Have a good day, Herbert, my little moppity zoo-bop."

Herbert wasn't sure if he liked it when she called him that or not.

His mom was always so cheerful when she said it that he didn't have

the heart to tell her.

The bus stop was just a couple of blocks away. Herbert was early,

so he took his time as he walked. The noisy bus arrived on time,

and Herbert quickly climbed up the steps and slid into a warm seat.

As the bus took off, the other kids were talking loudly, but Herbert

was quiet. He stared out the window. One morning he'd seen

a mother fox with two cubs running alongside the road.

These days the heavy traffic scared most animals away.

Herbert was just about to turn his head to look into his lunch bag
when he saw something falling out of the sky.
It was moving so fast that he couldn't see what it was.
A drone? A kite? A bird?
A meteorite? He thought he saw some dust fly up from behind
the brush, but he wasn't certain. He kept his eyes glued to the spot
where he thought the object had fallen, but the bus was almost
at school.

When the bus arrived at school and the bus driver opened
the doors, all the kids flowed out. Then Herbert did something that
would change his life. He turned left instead of right. No one
noticed that Herbert wasn't traveling with the crowd. He quickly
headed toward the brush. As Herbert headed closer and closer
to where the object had fallen, he felt as if he were in another
world. He heard the beautiful songs of many different types of birds.
He also heard crickets chirping. That sound always reminded him
of the meditation music his mom listened to in the evenings.
Suddenly Herbert heard a loud sound. It was coming from the bush
straight ahead of him. He approached cautiously. First he saw
a claw with huge talons. Then as he went around the bush,
he saw the head of a majestic golden eagle.

It seemed trapped. It was tangled in a rope. It was flapping

its wings with fright and had managed to ensnare itself even

further. *Wow!* Herbert thought to himself. *I've never seen an eagle*

up close before except in a zoo. It's huge. It must have a wingspan of

7 feet! The eagle stared into Herbert's eyes. Herbert would have

been scared, but he knew he was safe because the eagle couldn't

move. He could feel that the eagle was scared. He didn't want to get

any closer for fear that the eagle would do more damage

to its injured wing by flapping it. It made him feel sad to think that

the eagle might not be able to fly again. *I wonder what I should do,*

Herbert thought. *I think I should get one of my teachers to help.*

When Herbert finally got back to class he was horribly late. His teacher said, "Mr. Herbert Figmont Moppity Zoo-Bop, I'm glad you decided to grace us with your presence today. You are almost an hour late." The other kids laughed.

"I'm sorry, Mrs. Tuckleby, but I saw something drop out of the sky when we were driving in on the bus," Herbert said as his cheeks began to turn red.

"What was it?" one girl said, "A space alien in a saucer?"

"No, uh..." Herbert stammered as the class filled up with laughter. It was a golden eagle. I'm worried about it. It's hurt."

"Are you sure it was a *golden* eagle?" Mrs. Tuckleby asked with sudden interest.

"I'm sure," Herbert said. "It's all tangled up in a rope. It has huge wings."

Mrs. Tuckleby typed quickly on her computer and projected a photo on a screen. "Did it look like this?" The class began to ooh and aah at the photo of the massive bird.

Herbert quickly nodded his head.

Just then the principal, Mr. Harp, walked into the classroom.
He had heard Herbert talking from the hallway. He quietly chatted
with Mrs. Tuckleby. Then he squatted down next to Herbert's desk
and asked him some questions about where the eagle was. "I'll make
sure the animal rescue people come for your eagle," he whispered
to Herbert. Herbert felt so relieved.

The rest of the day went very slowly. Herbert tried to pay attention
to Mrs. Tuckleby, but his mind was on the golden eagle. He was
worried it might be scared when the rescue people approached it.

At the end of the school day, Mr. Harp came back to their classroom. He had someone else with him. Mrs. Tuckleby said, "Class we are finished with lessons for today, and we have a special guest. This is Mr. Jimmy Smith from the Talons Eagle Sanctuary. He wants to talk to you about the golden eagle Herbert found this morning."

The students began to talk to each other, but when Mr. Smith addressed the class they stopped. "Boys and girls, I have some good news. Thanks to Herbert's quick thinking we were able to rescue the golden eagle he found this morning. We will be able to fix his wing and he'll be able to fly again."

Herbert was so happy that the eagle would be able to fly again. He had a huge smile on his face. Mr. Smith continued his talk. "Do all of you know what the word endangered means?"

One girl raised her hand and said, "It means that there are less and less eagles."

"That's right," Mr. Smith said. "It's very important to save these majestic birds, but if you ever see one that is injured you should keep your distance. A golden eagle is a powerful bird of prey with sharp talons. Herbert did the right thing. He reported the injured eagle to an adult."

A boy raised his hand and asked, "How did the eagle get injured?"

"We don't know how he got tangled in the rope, but eagles are hurt by manmade things all the time. Sometimes they get into fights with other eagles too and get injured that way," Mr. Smith replied. "This eagle had a badly damaged wing that would not have healed on its own. Thanks to Herbert's kindness and compassion this amazing bird should heal up in a few weeks, and then we can set him free."

"I wish we could see the eagle in person," one girl said out loud.

Mrs. Tuckleby smiled. "You will all get to see Herbert's golden eagle next week. We're going to take a field trip to Talons Eagle Sanctuary. We'll meet the rescue people and see the eagle up close before they release him in the wild."

All the kids in class were excited and started to talk.

Then Mr. Smith took center stage again. "Before I leave today I have a special gift for Herbert."

Herbert stood up as Mr. Smith handed him a t-shirt with the words *Talons Eagle Sanctuary* and a picture of a golden eagle.

At the end of the day as the students left school they all wanted to be near Herbert and ask him questions about the golden eagle.

"What you did was so cool, Herbert," one girl said as she smiled.

"Yeah, I think I would have been scared of the talons," one of the boys said.

"I can't wait until we go next week and see how he's doing," Herbert said.

When the bus dropped him off, Herbert ran home. He couldn't wait to tell his parents about his exciting day over dinner.

After he told them everything, his mom said, "Well, I don't like that you were late for school, but you acted responsibly."

"Yes, son, we're very proud of you," his dad said. "I like your t-shirt too. It's good to have memories of special days."

Herbert just smiled. He felt he could soar just like the golden eagle.

Lightning Source UK Ltd.
Milton Keynes UK
UKHW051134071222
413511UK00002B/47